S0-BNJ-606

BAILEY J. RUSSELL • NEIL EVANS

THE HAUNTING
OF Hawthorne Harbor

BOOK 6 : THE FIRE

Claw

An Imprint of Magic Wagon
abdobooks.com

abdobooks.com

Published by Magic Wagon, a division of ABDO, PO Box 398166, Minneapolis, Minnesota 55439. Copyright © 2021 by Abdo Consulting Group, Inc. International copyrights reserved in all countries. No part of this book may be reproduced in any form without written permission from the publisher. Claw™ is a trademark and logo of Magic Wagon.

Printed in the United States of America, North Mankato, Minnesota.
082020
012021

Written by Bailey J. Russell
Illustrated by Neil Evans
Edited by Tamara L. Britton
Art Direction by Victoria Bates

Library of Congress Control Number: 2020930096

Publisher's Cataloging-in-Publication Data

Names: Russell, Bailey J., author. | Evans, Neil, illustrator.
Title: The fire / by Bailey J. Russell ; illustrated by Neil Evans.
Description: Minneapolis, Minnesota : Magic Wagon, 2021. | Series: The
    haunting of Hawthorne Harbor; book 6
Summary: The Portal in Hawthorne Harbor is opening. Aaron Hawthorne
    must keep it closed. He plans the ritual and counts on his nephew John
    to assist him. Then John threatens Aaron's life, and Aaron admits what he
    has feared. That's not really John pointing the gun at him. But if it's not
    John, who is it?
Identifiers: ISBN 9781532138416 (lib. bdg.) | ISBN 9781532139130 (ebook) |
    ISBN 9781532139499 (Read-to-Me ebook)
Subjects: LCSH: High school students--Juvenile fiction. | Ghosts--Juvenile
    fiction. | Rituals--Juvenile fiction. | Mistaken identity--Juvenile fiction. |
    Supernatural--Juvenile fiction. | Mystery and detective stories--Juvenile
    fiction.
Classification: DDC [FIC]--dc23

Table of CONTENTS

FIC
KUSS

chapter ONE

When Jane woke Thursday morning, she winced at a sudden pain. On the underside of her wrist was a thin line of dried blood. It wasn't a deep cut, but it stung when she pressed her finger to it. Jane couldn't remember cutting herself last night.

It was only five in the morning. There was an abundance of time before school started. Jane knew she wouldn't be able to go back to sleep, so she started some coffee.

When she went to get a coffee mug out of the cupboard, Jane glanced at the cookie jar—her grandfather's makeshift urn—where it still sat on the kitchen counter. She really should do something with that.

Jane still wasn't sure what had possessed

her to put the small piece of bone in her pocket. Was this just the first of even more eccentric things she would do, now that she was a thirtysomething woman who had moved back to her childhood home? Furthermore, at what age were you no longer considered an independent woman and relegated to spinsterhood? Jane was afraid she had already passed that milestone.

As she stared at the cookie jar, waiting for the coffee to finish brewing, Jane noticed a large smudge of what must have been ash on the side. Jane walked over and leaned in close. The smudge curved around the body of the jar like a rather large thumbprint. She clearly remembered wiping down the jar after she first cleaned up the horrible mess of ash.

The only time she had opened the lid since had been to drop the fragment of her grandfather's wayward bone shard inside.

Even then, she had not touched the ash. At least, she didn't think she had . . . could she really have walked around with traces of her grandfather on her hands and not known it? Jane made a little choking sound that was something between a gag and a gasp and held her hands out in front of her. Perfectly clean.

She really needed to give the whole house another scouring before she had any more guests over. Aaron had come in to use the bathroom last night before walking home. She hoped that he hadn't noticed the mouse problem or the pervading smell of cigar smoke. Her embarrassment was starting to win out over her smugness by a landslide.

Jane carried the cookie jar over to the sink and rinsed it clean again. She wondered how much of her grandfather would eventually end up washed out with the dishwater to the Puget Sound. She thought that would be rather nice—to just float out with the tides and mingle with the kelp and the schools of fish.

Maybe she would go scatter her grandfather's ashes one of these weekends, before the weather completely turned. What would she do with him otherwise? Just put Grandpa up on a shelf for the next five or six decades until her ashes joined him in her own dreary urn?

She left her father's car in the driveway and walked the twenty minutes to the high school, enjoying the brisk morning air and the growing light of a day not yet fully formed. It still needs to rise, she had thought, like bread dough. Like my life.

Jane walked past the great house she knew belonged to Principal Hawthorne. The house itself was surrounded by a tall, iron fence, and she imagined that the yard inside was perfectly manicured. There was a light on in one of the second-story windows. She stopped and stared up, hoping that no one was looking down at her. It was still quite dark, so she didn't think she had to worry.

Jane had heard that Aaron's wife had left him several years earlier. She wondered if he was often alone in that big house or if some of the women in town kept him company. The thought that she might be just one of a string of women attracted to him made her frown. But she couldn't really blame them—these phantom women who now haunted the edges of her mind. He certainly was handsome.

When Jane arrived at the school, she saw a car parked on the far side of the lot. It was still fairly dark to see for sure, but the car looked black and quite expensive. She used her new key to unlock the school and stepped inside. The air felt warm in the entryway—warmer than she would have expected. Perhaps the heat had been left on at night? That seemed quite wasteful.

As she walked down the still-dark hall, Jane rolled up the sleeves on her cardigan and fanned her face. It was actually quite stifling. She might have to open a window.

When she reached her classroom, she nearly gasped in surprise. John Hawthorne was sitting at his desk with his head in his hands. He looked like he was sleeping. Jane paused, wondering if she should wake the boy. She took a step toward him, then hesitated. She could see the bare nape of his neck and the slow rise and fall of his shoulders.

John startled at her touch, and then jerked his head up. For an instant, John looked at Jane with an expression somewhere between confusion and fear. His brows furrowed darkly over his green eyes, and he looked

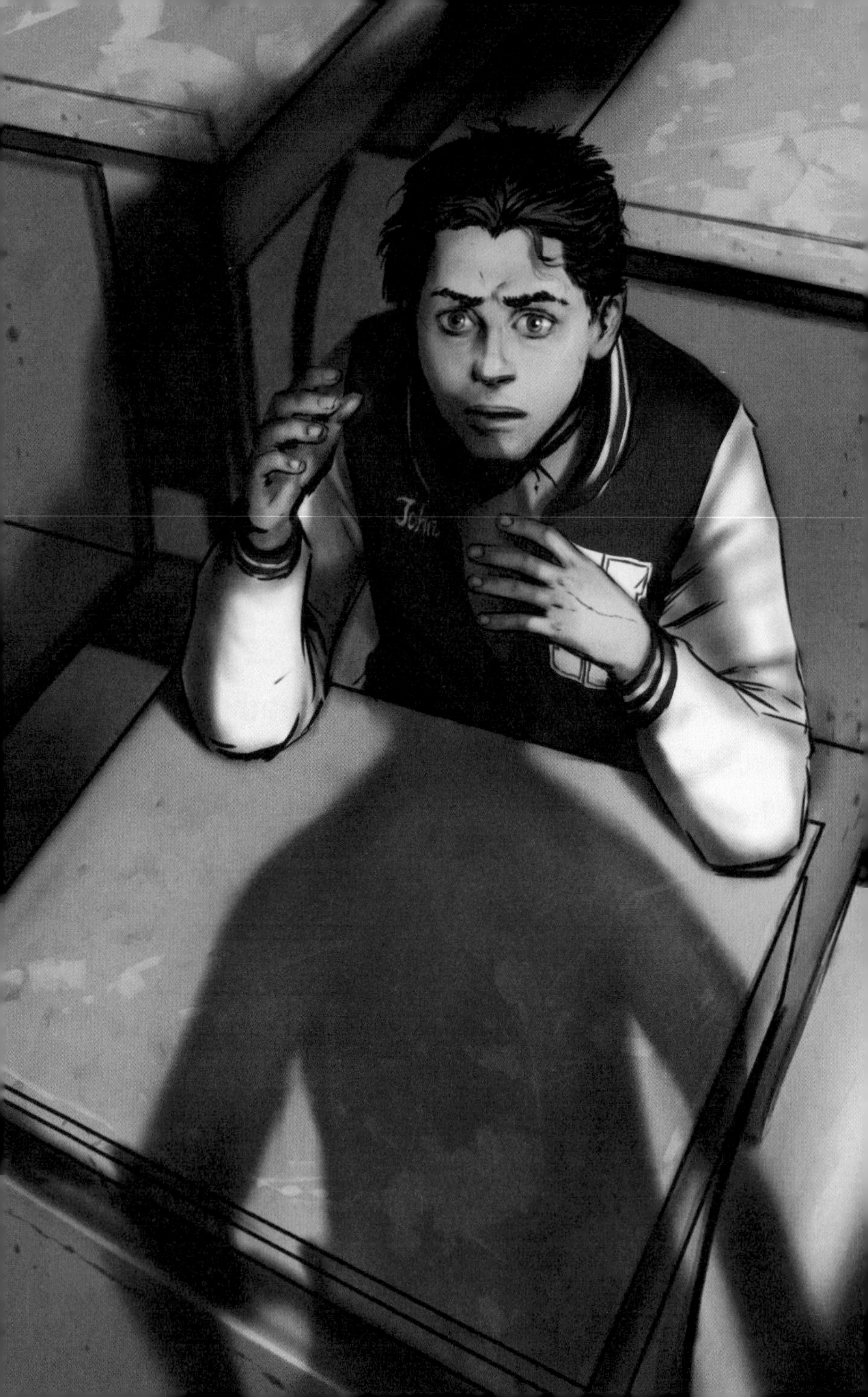
John

right through Jane—as though he could see something right behind her. Something horrible.

Then his expression changed so quickly that Jane could almost have imagined the strange, fearful look. He smiled and stretched out his arms, yawning. "Oh. Hi, Miss Owens. Was I sleeping?"

"Why are you in my classroom? It is six o'clock in the morning." She hoped he wouldn't ask why she had arrived at school so early—as though she had been caught doing something indecent. But why shouldn't she be here? Students had no idea how early a teacher needed to get to class. For all he knew, Jane arrived at this time every day.

Granted, she had brought along a copy of *Jane Eyre* and was planning to just read for several hours in the sterile calm of the classroom—enjoying every moment before the first students arrived. And, to be honest, she had started to hope that Aaron might stop by her classroom while she was all alone.

John's gaze still seemed somewhat unfocused—not quite meeting her eyes. Jane hoped he wasn't on drugs. He stood up, scooting his chair back with a loud scrape. "I have to go meet my uncle. See you later, Miss Owens."

"In two hours, Mr. Hawthorne."

John gave her a causal grin, then walked stiffly toward the door, his shoulders slightly hunched. Jane hoped she was imagining things.

After the strange, cocky boy left, Jane collapsed into her own chair. It was uncomfortable, but solid. The heat seemed to suddenly dissipate, leaving her shivering in the empty room.

chapter
TWO

When John woke up in the middle of the night on Wednesday, he wasn't actually sure that he was awake. He felt something cold press against his lips, and when he opened his eyes, he found Katie's face inches from his own. She gave him a huge smile—like she was just so happy to see him that she couldn't hold it inside.

Katie kissed him again, cutting off the words he was trying to say: *What are you doing here?* Katie had never been up to his room before, and certainly not in the middle of the night. She climbed under the covers and lay down next to him. Everywhere her skin touched his, John felt like he was on fire—she was so cold. John pulled her closer to him, brushing her damp hair out of his eyes.

Was he dreaming? He must be dreaming.

"Katie," John finally said, murmuring into her ear. "What are you doing here?"

"Tell me you love me," she whispered.

"I love you." John realized that he had never said that to her before. He was pretty sure that he meant it. But why was she so cold? His teeth chattered while he kissed her again.

She smiled at him—her teeth caught the moonlight. "Tell me you love me," she said again. John was shivering so violently that he almost couldn't say the words. "I love you, Katie. I love you." Now that he was no longer caught up in the moment, the other John—the John who had been observing this encounter—spoke up. *Why is she here? In your room? Why is she so cold?*

Finally, John couldn't lie beside her for

another moment. He was freezing. As he sat up, Katie frowned at him.

"Tell me you love me," she repeated. There was something different about her voice. He had never heard this strange, insistent tone before. She was almost growling. "Tell me you love me," she said again, louder this time. She was going to wake up his mother.

"Quiet!" John hissed, as the other John's anger and impatience surged up from his stomach.

Why was she here? What was she doing here? John's head began to ache again, and he felt that familiar pulling sensation, like his vision was being split in two. Two Johns looking at Katie's strange smile.

Katie sat up, her hair falling across her chest. Her face was all hard lines and shadow in the moonlight. Deep caverns for her eyes.

"Tell me you love me," she said again, and

John reached out and grabbed her, his fingers digging into the curves of her shoulders. He held her at arm's length, and the cold spread up his hands into his arms. John felt like he was floating above his body, watching himself shake his girlfriend so hard that her head snapped back and forth. He watched himself slap her across the face.

"Be quiet," he hissed again.

Katie reached out her hand and shoved it into his chest. Her hand vanished up to her pale wrist, sticking out just below the center of his rib cage. She was still smiling, but a smile that John had never seen before. Katie's lips were pulled back to reveal the glint of her teeth. It actually looked more like a grimace than a smile.

"You. Love. Me," she said, slowly. With each word, the air seemed to squeeze from his lungs. She must have had her fist wrapped

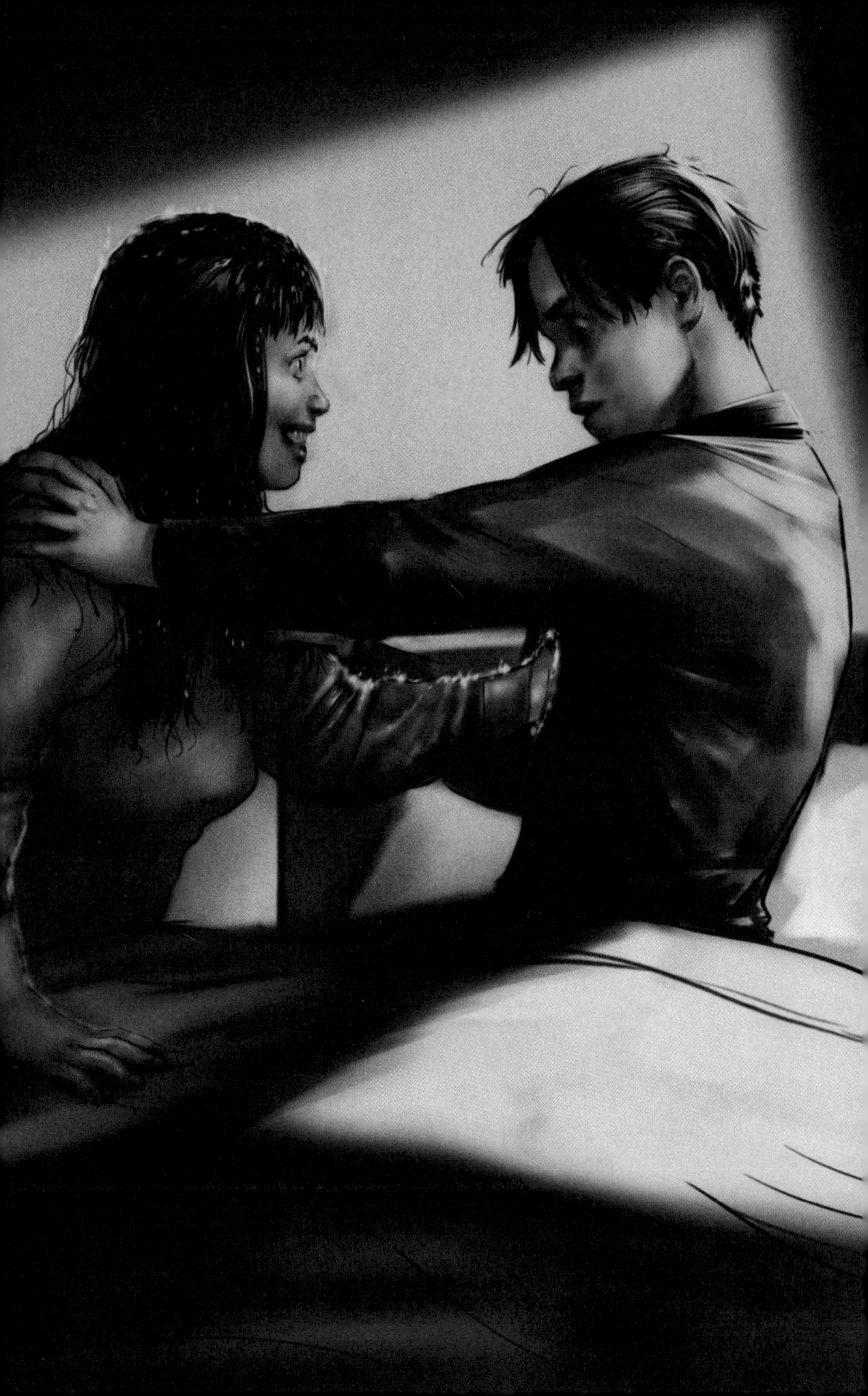

around his heart. He closed his eyes and reached out for her with his mind—with the same reflex that might cause a drowning person to inhale water instead of air.

John didn't pause to think about what he was doing, or what it meant. Grasping the claws of his concentration firmly around her body, John scattered each particle of Katie's ghost to the four corners of his room.

John opened his eyes and slapped his hand over his heart. He took a deep, gulping breath. The skin on his chest was numb, but he could feel the slow, steady beat of his heart vibrate through his body.

The light from the moon puddled over his bed, and his rumpled sheets seemed to twist and pulse. He held his hands out in front of him. The moonlight made them look different, too. His hands almost looked like they were glowing.

He closed his eyes again. The blood flowed slowly through his veins, and his head swam. *Did that just happen?* That was John's first coherent thought, once the cold started to seep from his body, and he could breathe again without a burning panic throbbing in his throat. *Was I dreaming?*

As John sat on his bed, still staring wide-eyed into the dark of his room, the urgency of the past few minutes started to fade. Maybe it was just a dream. John picked up the pillow where he had just seen Katie rest her head. He pressed it to his face and inhaled. Katie smelled like perfume, and sometimes oranges. The pillow case smelled like nothing—or maybe just his Brylcreem.

"It was only a dream." John said the words out loud, blinking into the shadows. There was something final about hearing his own voice—like a soap bubble popping. "Only a dream," he said again, and he sank his fingernails into the skin just above his heart. Even when his nails broke the skin, leaving behind bleeding half-moons, he felt nothing.

The first thing Aaron had ever taught John about ghosts was to not feel sorry for them. The other rules and lessons—how to guard your mind against a ghost; to use a knife until you could use your mind to feel the gritty, sticky substance that held them together and rip it apart—all of these came later. First and foremost, John had to understand that ghosts should never be pitied.

They had already had their chance on earth, and feeling sorry for a ghost would not bring the person back to life. The person and the ghost were two separate things. Crying over a dead thing would only make you weak.

As John lay awake, trying to decide if what just happened with Katie had all been a dream, he thought back to the first ghost he was supposed to destroy but couldn't. John was twelve years old at the time. He could still picture himself standing over the dead girl, the knife in his hand.

The ghost was kneeling on the ground, her hands covering her head. She didn't seem to know she was dead—that was the part that John couldn't get out of his head, even after all these years. She looked afraid.

The ghost wore a pale blue dress that was already splattered with blood. Before she covered her face, John saw a slice down her cheek and dark bruises around her neck. John should have just done it himself, but there was something about the girl that made him afraid to try.

He didn't want to mess it up. He didn't want her to be in any more pain.

When his uncle took the knife from John's

hand and approached the ghost, she had looked right at Aaron and put up her hands. His uncle kicked her in the stomach, and she doubled over.

"Like this," Aaron had called back to John. "Catch them by surprise. That's the best way." Then he jammed his knee into her face. John had to look away while his uncle held her by the hair and forced her to her knees.

Ghosts weren't real. They weren't people. It didn't matter how you destroyed them, as long as they were gone. But John couldn't forget that smile on his uncle's face when he plunged the knife into the back of the girl's neck as she cowered before him.

"You see," Aaron had told John, handing him back the knife. "You can't feel sorry for them, or you'll hesitate. If you hesitate, you'll die. Do you want to be dead? Like your father?"

John had shaken his head and clutched the knife to his chest. He didn't want to be dead, and he especially didn't want to be like his father. His father was a coward.

chapter THREE

When the morning light started to trickle through his window, John couldn't lie in bed anymore. He got up—before his mother, even—and drove himself to school. He needed to talk to his uncle.

John decided that it had definitely been a dream. He had had realistic dreams ever since he could remember. Sometimes he dreamed about a light that was so bright that it melted the skin from his hands. John had heard that you couldn't actually experience pain in a dream. But he knew he felt an intense, scorching pain that was as white as a star clenched in his fists.

As John drove, he inspected the red, angry-looking cut on the top of his hand. He tried again to remember how he had gotten it. The cut almost looked like a cat scratch.

The door was locked, but that didn't bother John. His uncle had given him a key a few weeks before school started. In case they needed to meet in his office, Aaron had said, though that had seemed unlikely at the time to John. They always had their lessons at Aaron's house.

His uncle wasn't there yet. John didn't want to wait in Aaron's office, so he went to his history class, which would be empty at that time in the morning. Something about the classroom just felt right, he thought, as he sat in his desk and stared up at the chalkboard.

As John waited for his uncle to arrive, he began to grow tired. His head drooped. Before he knew it, Miss Owens was shaking him awake. As soon as he opened his eyes, he saw a ghost with dark goggles standing right behind Miss Owens. John almost shouted for her to run.

The ghost had placed its hand on her shoulder, though she didn't seem to feel it. Her face, however, looked blotchy, and there were beads of sweat along her scalp, where her hair was pulled back into her usual severe bun.

John had never met another person, besides his uncle, who was a Seer. But that didn't mean that ghosts couldn't see them. He didn't shout, and he didn't warn her. He just smiled and left as soon as he could.

As John left the classroom, the ghost followed—exactly what he'd hoped the ghost would do. John could feel the ghost behind him like a wall of flame—the skin on the back of his neck crinkling with the heat. What kind of a ghost gave off heat like that? Katie had been so cold . . . but that was just a dream, right? How could Katie be a ghost?

Once John had lured the ghost out into the empty hallway, he turned and reached out and touched the ghost's face. He jerked his hand back as though burnt. He was burnt, John realized. The tips of his fingers had turned an ashen white.

"Ouch!" John hissed, and the ghost cocked his head back at him. The ghost's face, beneath the goggles, looked very familiar. John was sure he had seen this man before. John tried to see through the goggles to the man beneath, but he couldn't. They were just black, like the stuff Native Americans used to make arrowheads. Obsidian—that was it.

He slowly walked to his uncle's office and opened the door with the same key. The office smelled like incense and was chilly until the ghost entered the room. Then it was hot— almost unbearably hot. What was this ghost?

John reached out his mind again and tried to grab hold of the ghost but again couldn't. He was too . . . slippery. That was the only way to describe it. John sat in his uncle's chair, and the ghost leaned against the wall opposite him. There were flames in the ghost's goggles, and John noticed small, black marks forming around the ghost's shoulder—as though the wall itself was starting to burn.

"Who are you?" John asked the ghost. He had never met a ghost who could actually hold a true conversation with him, but some, like the woman in the theater, could speak a little. They could answer a few questions.

The ghost smiled. His teeth looked dark, and slick with something. Blood? John couldn't tell. The ghost licked his lips, and then made a sound that was something like a deep breath or a sigh.

"Release me," the ghost said. His voice was

deep and gravelly, and John felt like some nerve deep within his body had been struck and set to vibrate. Where was his uncle?

"Who are you?" John asked again. The ghost didn't speak this time, but continued to stare back at John. The ghost wore dark coveralls, and they looked like they were charred. Even for work clothes, his coveralls and boots looked old, as though he had stepped out of a picture from the Great Depression.

John tried again to feel the ghost. He concentrated on the man's throat and reached out with an imaginary hand. John tried to catch hold of the ghost's trachea and the fragile sinews and veins in the ghost's neck. Sometimes that was the most effective way to subdue a ghost—grab them by the neck.

Once again, it felt like John was trying to claw at wet glass. He couldn't find a place to hold on. The ghost smiled at him—a mocking smile, John thought—and shook his head. This ghost felt stronger than any John had ever felt before.

"Let me go," the ghost said. John wanted to cover his ears to block out the echo of the ghost's voice.

They waited like that—John's eyes locked on the flat, unblinking goggles of the ghost—until his uncle arrived. Aaron opened his office door and frowned at John in his chair.

"What are you doing here?" Aaron asked.

"Aaron," John began, still looking across the room to the ghost. "I found something I thought you'd like to see." He tried to keep his voice calm, but he felt like he was slipping off the edge of a cliff he hadn't even known existed until that moment.

"Can you actually see him?" Aaron asked, gesturing towards the ghost. "You can, can't you? I can't, isn't that strange? I can feel him though . . . the heat of him. The power. But I can't see him. What does he look like? Is he covered with burns?"

John couldn't take his eyes off the ghost.

"No," John managed to say. "I mean, he doesn't look burnt. He looks . . . burning. Everything he touches seems to burn."

The ghost smiled more broadly, and John shuddered. "Can you, you know, take care of him now? It isn't working when I try."

Aaron shook his head. "Of course it's not. You're not strong enough."

John's head throbbed seemingly in response to Aaron's words. *You'll be stronger than him*, the voice in his head whispered. *We'll be stronger.*

"Aren't you going to do something?" John managed to say out loud.

Aaron didn't answer his question. "Why weren't you at our lesson yesterday?"

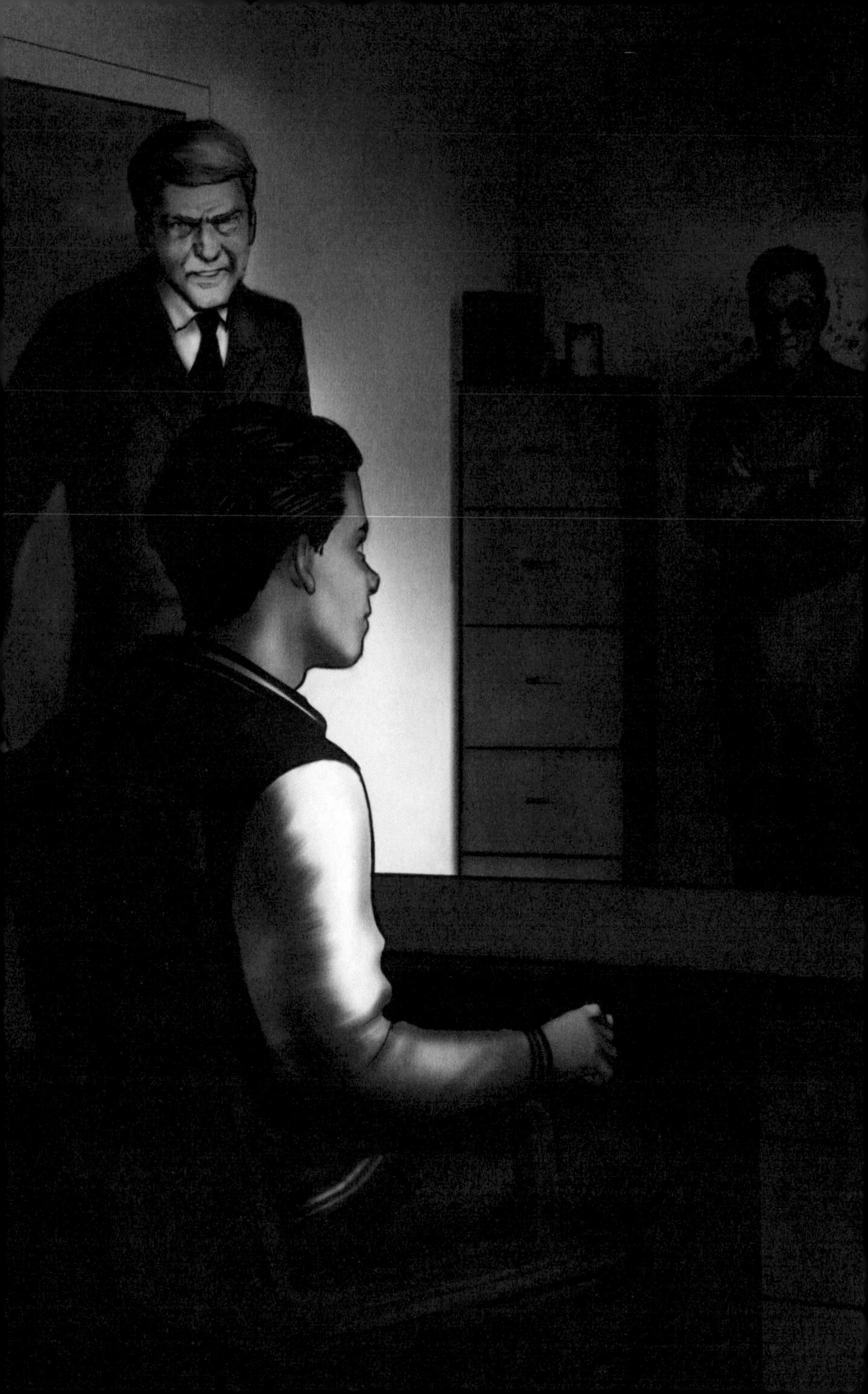

"Is that important right now?" John watched as the ghost crossed his arms and looked at Aaron, as though he was also waiting for the answer.

"It is actually incredibly important. Where were you yesterday?"

"I took Katie to the movies, okay? Can we deal with this . . . situation now?" John didn't like to say the word *ghost* in front of actual ghosts. They didn't always know that they were dead, and it could just make them mad.

For a moment John considered telling his uncle about the dream he had last night. Even with the burning ghost staring at him, he was impatient to tell someone . . . to hear his uncle say, "Don't worry, it was just a dream."

Aaron crossed the room and took John's face in his hand. "I told you that girl was nothing but a distraction." He gestured to the ghost. "If you had come to your lesson yesterday, I would have told you about this ghost. I would have told you about my plans. Our plans. But you couldn't even show up. Is that the kind of Seer you will be when I'm gone? Is that who you want to be?"

John had only heard Aaron use the word *Seer* a few times. Aaron's brother, John's father, had been a Seer. Aaron was a Seer, too, but not as strong a one as his brother had been.

Not as strong as you are going to be, the voice whispered again.

"No, sir," John managed to say through clenched teeth.

Aaron let go of his nephew's face, and then patted his cheek. "You're going to be all right, my boy. I wish it didn't have to be this way. I wish you didn't make me do these things."

What things? John wondered as he left his uncle's office and went to go wait for school to start in his car. In his mind he saw Katie's

face again, how she looked the night before—
full of shadows.

What things does Aaron do?

chapter FOUR

John didn't see Katie at school that day. He went to her parents' house after school, but her mother didn't know where she was. She thought Katie had come home after they already went to bed, which was very unlike her, and then left before they got up. She asked John to have her come straight home if he saw her.

John left Katie's house, got back in his car, and started driving. It had to have been a dream. It had to be . . . unless it wasn't.

Unless Katie was lying dead somewhere.

He tried to remember what Katie had looked like in the dark. Were there any marks on her? Any sign of how she had been killed? Her skin was so smooth—unmarred by any wounds. He just remembered how cold she had been. But . . . it had to have been a dream, because people didn't just die like that.

Except, that dark, raspy part of his mind reminded him, *they do. All the time.*

John drove to his uncle's house for his lesson because he didn't really know what else to do. He couldn't exactly go to the police and say that he saw Katie's ghost.

He let himself in and went straight to Aaron's study. A plate of chocolate chip cookies was sitting on his uncle's desk. Alice had certainly gone home already, but she always remembered to leave a treat for John. He was glad that Alice wasn't there. Who knew what his uncle was up to.

John didn't have to wait very long before his uncle arrived.

"On time for once. Good," Aaron said, pausing to look into John's face. "You look terrible. How have you been sleeping?"

John could have said the same thing about Aaron. His uncle had huge bags under his eyes, and the lines around his mouth were more severe than usual.

"Actually—" John started to say, but Aaron cut him off.

"Tomorrow is a big day for us," Aaron said. "You read the book I gave you, right?"

"The newspapers? Sure." John hadn't actually read them. He had given them a cursory glance, but that was all. He had other things on his mind. Like Katie. "But I was hoping—"

"Then you know what is happening tomorrow. You understand, right? What I have to do? What we have to do?" Aaron had pulled out his desk chair but didn't move to sit in it. He was waiting for John to speak.

John shook his head. "What?"

"The Accident," Aaron said slowly, "happened fifty years ago tomorrow. I was hoping you would show some initiative—some imagination—and figure it out on your own. The way your father did. That you would finally show me that you have some of his spirit in you, the kind you'll need to take up the mantle once I'm gone. But I'll spell it out for you. The Accident was a ritual. A sacrifice. The men who died . . . their deaths kept the Portal closed for another fifty years. The Portal which is now opening."

"Oh," John said, but it sounded more like the sound he might make had he just been punched in the stomach. A sacrifice? "Why didn't you tell me this before?"

"Why didn't I tell a child that a Portal to the Dead was opening, and we needed to perform a ritual to keep it closed?" Aaron laughed. "When should I have told you? When you were old enough to drive? When you were old enough to drink?"

John shook his head. "You could have told me at any point. You had to wait until now?"

"You didn't need to know before now. You know I . . . I won't be here forever. I just need to know that you can do it. That you can carry this with you for the next fifty years. That you will perform the next ritual. I need to know that you are capable of this on your own."

"What is the ritual? What are we supposed to do?"

"We aren't doing anything . . . not this time. I'm doing the ritual this time. But you'll learn." Aaron leaned against the desk and didn't look at John, but down at his own hands instead. "You will do it next time. In fifty years."

John could hear the whispers again, racing

and twisting in his skull like rushing water: *he lies, he lies, he lies, he lies.*

John wondered if they were right.

Thursday had gone by achingly slow for Jane. She found herself on several occasions staring silently at the students, her mind completely empty. It was kind of like forgetting your lines in a play, she imagined. And the students had stared back just as vacantly. They seemed to feel the end of summer. Many of the symptoms were the same: irritability, sluggishness, an inability to concentrate.

Jane sometimes wondered what the point of schools were. Were children really meant to be cooped up all day, hidden away from the sun? Were teachers?

Aaron smiled when they passed in the hall, but he didn't exactly seek her out. At the end of the day, Jane walked home and finally went through her father's books. She didn't really sort them, but just dumped them all into an empty box.

Among his books she found something interesting. There were a few old newspaper clippings trapped between the pages of an old, musty dictionary.

The clippings were old, starting in 1915. There was an article about plans for a new school. The land, the article read, had been generously donated by brothers Theodore and Ethan Hawthorne. Another article mentioned that human bones had been found on the land. They showed signs of having been burnt. The local authorities thought that they were Native American bones, possibly from a funeral pyre. One lurid hypothesis was that the Native Americans had taken part in some kind of ritualistic sacrifice.

Jane wondered why she had never heard about the bones before. There were so many—

at least fifteen individual skeletons had been uncovered. Surely that was worth learning about in history class.

Five other news articles covered plans for the new school up to the time of the Accident. For some reason, no one had bothered to keep a clipping about that terrible day.

That was when Jane thought to look in the front of the dictionary. There, on the inside of the front cover, she read the name. W. C. Owens. So it wasn't her father who had kept the clippings. He may have never known that they were there. It was her grandfather who had kept them when he started working on the school. That was why the clippings stopped. He wasn't around to collect them anymore.

Jane had never exactly grieved for a grandfather she had never known—one who would have surely been dead by now anyway had he not been killed fifty years earlier. But now she swallowed back tears as she sat on the floor, with the clippings that her grandfather had collected with his own hands spread out around her.

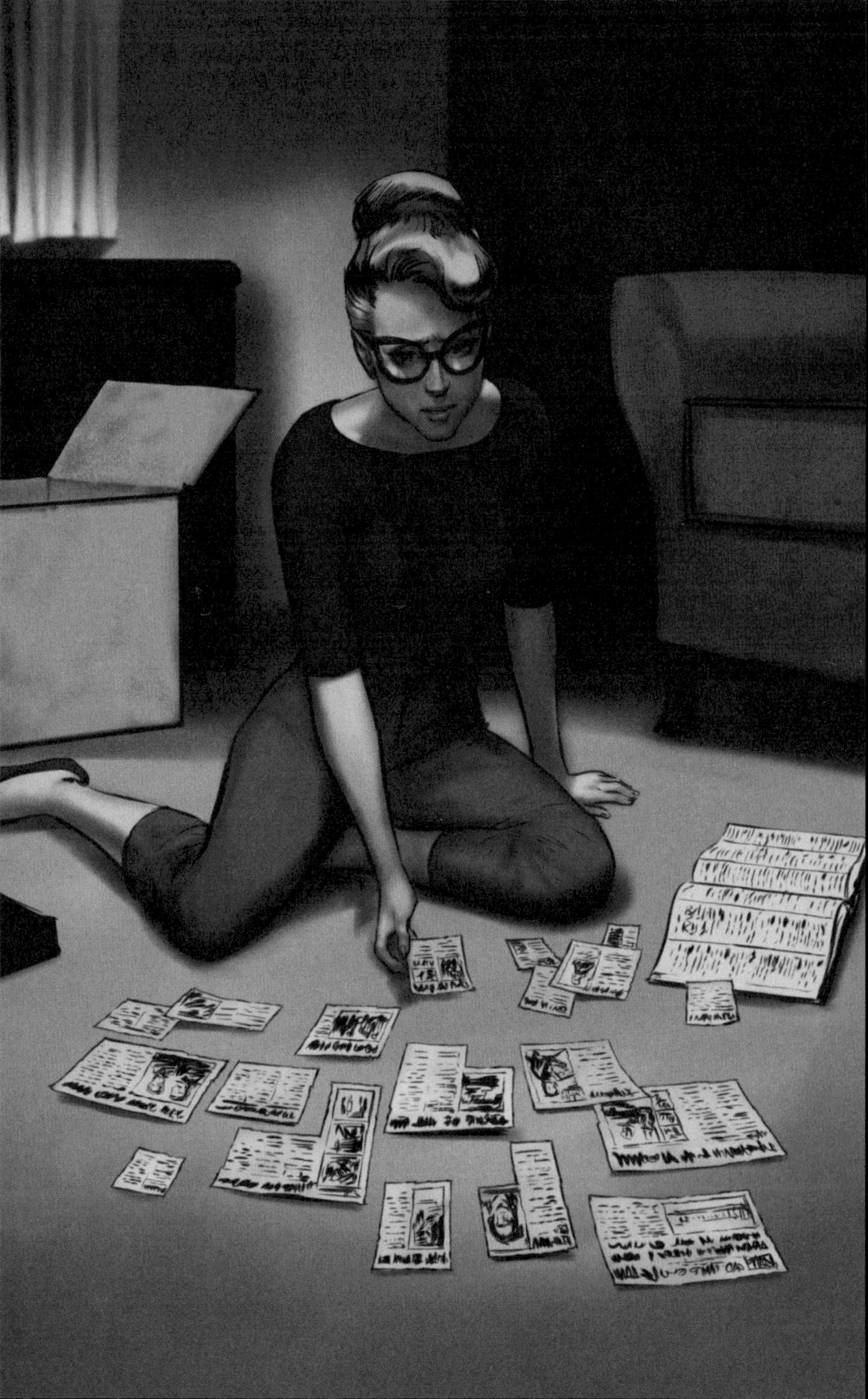

chapter FIVE

That night, John returned to his uncle's house after dark and parked three blocks away. Even if his uncle could have seen his car from his window, the pitch-black paint job would have masked it in the shadows. It was almost one in the morning, but John didn't feel tired at all. The moon was humming in his blood.

Sometimes, even before John saw a ghost, he could taste it in the air. A dusty, iron taste—like a mixture of dirt and blood. It was almost a smell, but it filled both his nose and mouth, nearly making him gag. John had asked his uncle, once, if Aaron could taste ghosts. His uncle just shook his head, with a mystified expression on his face.

"Fascinating!" Aaron had said. John remembered that clearly. Fascinating, like John was a science experiment. But no, it turned out, Aaron could not taste ghosts. So there was one more thing that John could do better than his uncle.

You're stronger than he is, the voice in his head whispered again. *You were always the strong one. Like your father.*

When John pushed open the gate to his uncle's property, it swung open silently. He shut it behind him and walked in the grass beside the gravel path so his steps wouldn't make a sound.

Deep shadows cut across the path. John tried to avoid any fallen sticks that might snap underfoot. It wasn't until he quietly walked up the front stairs that he tasted the iron tinge of blood on his tongue. The hair on the back of John's neck stood on end, and his stomach tightened. John looked all around, but didn't see anything.

Keep going, the voice in his head scolded him. *You have to keep going.*

The door was locked, but John had a key. He let himself inside, and then held his breath as he closed the door behind him. For some reason, John was suddenly sure that the house was empty. There was a stillness—a perfect calm in the air that made John think of abandoned kingdoms and cities overgrown by jungle vines. Forgotten civilizations. But the house always felt empty to some extent, even when his uncle was inside. There were too many rooms. Too much stagnant air in the corners of the house.

The taste of blood still lingered in his mouth and stung his nose. He started to sweat, even though he knew that the huge, drafty house was cold. John began to wonder if Katie's ghost had broken something inside of him when she grabbed his heart. Had any of that actually happened? Could it have been a dream?

The door to Aaron's study was locked, and John didn't have a key this time. He rested his head on the wood door and took a deep breath. Then, almost without thinking, John took hold of the doorknob and held it in both hands. He heard a crackling sound, like static electricity. His fingers began to tingle.

John watched the doorknob begin to glow beneath his hands. He could see the bones of his fingers beneath his illuminated skin. What was happening? Things don't just start glowing when you touch them. But that part of his mind grew muted until he could barely hear himself think. The crackling sound intensified, and something inside the doorknob made a snapping sound. John turned the knob, and the door swung open.

The moon brightened one side of the room in a colorless light. The walls were lined with books, and John tried to find the shelf—the one that held the secret compartment.

What? John frowned and clutched his head with both hands. John had never thought about any secret compartment before that instant. Was he losing his mind? But he knew—just like he knew the color of the sky or the scent of roses—that his uncle was hiding something. And he knew where to look.

John could have turned on a light, but that might have given him away in case his uncle came home. He still wasn't sure why he knew his uncle wasn't in the house.

Trust me, the voice in his head whispered. *I know what I'm doing.*

After running his fingers beneath the lip of several shelves—his shoulder throbbing with the motion—John felt a latch. He pressed in on the latch and pulled. The shelf swung out and to the side, revealing a small compartment. There was an old-looking book inside.

A thrill ran through John, and he smiled broadly. He felt a sudden rush of pride at the sight of the book—a protectiveness. He remembered the weight of it in his hands. But that didn't make sense. John had never seen the book before. He shook his head, trying to make sense of the warring memories in his mind.

As he picked up the book—a slim, dusty-smelling volume—John felt a cold object against the back of his hand. Something metal. The compartment was deeper than he had thought at first, and he had to stand on his tiptoes to reach all the way to the very back corner. Before John closed the compartment, he pulled out two more items. The first was a wooden cigar box with something inside that rattled when he picked it up.

The second was a gun.

When John left the house and walked into the cold night air, the heat from his uncle's house seemed to follow him. And the box, clutched beneath his arm, felt heavier than it should be, almost as though something living had been forced into its confines. *A genie in a bottle*, he suddenly thought.

Back in his car, John opened the wooden box. He had stowed the gun in the bottom of his bag, beneath the books. He had never fired a gun before, but when he first held it in his hand there was something unmistakably familiar about the heft of it. John knew that he could use it, if he needed to.

If Aaron makes us, the voice in his head whispered.

Inside the box, John found a few pieces of what he thought at first were shards of broken pottery. When he moved them around, an electric sensation pulsed up his wrist, the same feeling he had when holding the glowing doorknob.

John shook the shards into the palm of his hand, and holding them up to the dome light in his car, he took a closer look. They were white, with a dusting of rust or dried blood. There were also a few strands of hair that could have been silver or pale blond scattered among the broken pieces.

As John poured the shards from one hand to the other—wondering what value his uncle had placed on a broken dish or mug—John tasted blood in his mouth again. Then he felt something so hot on the back of his neck that he yelped in surprise and almost spilled the shards onto the floor.

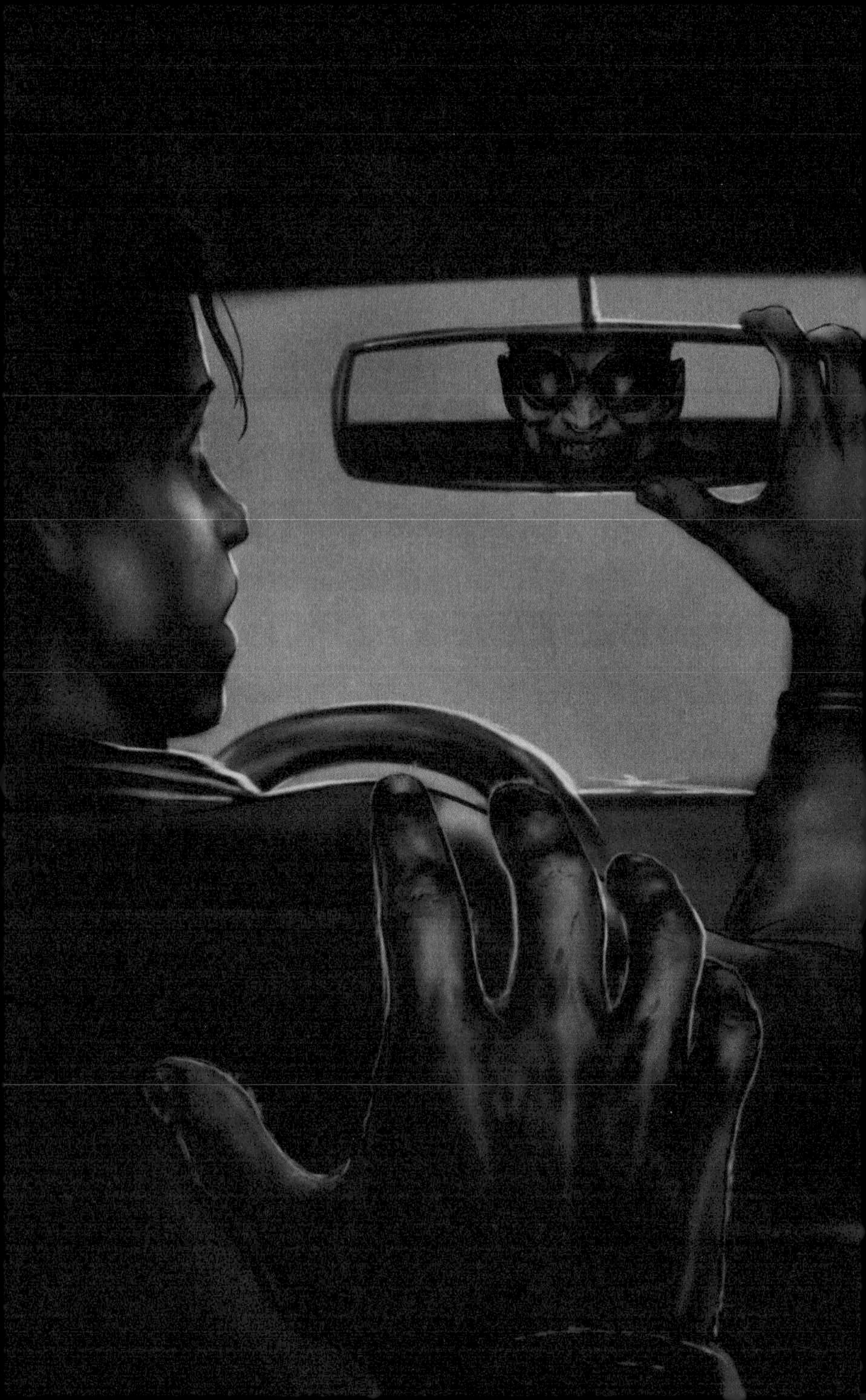

Glancing up to the rearview mirror, John saw a man's face in the back seat of his car. It was the man with the dark goggles, and a light was flickering in their depths. His hand was raised and hovered just inches from the back of John's neck.

John almost dropped the shards. Bones, he suddenly realized. The ghost's bones. But he closed his hand around them instead. He whispered, "Stop," in a shaky, hoarse voice. The ghost drew his own hand back and vanished.

He held his closed fist in front of him for a long time—staring in the mirror at the back seat of the car. The ghost didn't return. Finally, when the cool night air displaced the heat that had come from the ghost, John lowered his hand and returned the bones to the box.

Fascinating, John thought to himself, a smile slowly spreading across his face.

John started the car, knowing that he couldn't let his uncle find him there. Then he drove. He didn't return home, but rather made a wide circle around the town, driving past the theater on Main Street, and then up to the narrow back roads that had no streetlights.

He didn't realize where he was going until he reached the abandoned bunkers. Soldiers used to be stationed there, during World War II, with huge guns meant to protect Puget Sound from enemy ships and submarines. Now it was a park, and people could walk through the long, concrete tunnels and climb up to the battlements where the soldiers used to stand guard.

John got out of the car and took his book bag with him. There was a path you could walk that wove down to a thin, rocky beach below the bunkers. Katie had shown him this spot on one of their first dates. She made him a picnic, and he held her arm while she slowly picked her way over the uneven, root-snarled path in her slippery shoes. It was a place that was hidden from view unless you took that slight, twisting path. Their secret.

chapter
SIX

Katie had been cold in the dream that had to have been a dream, but wasn't. Cold, but otherwise the same. After he stepped out of his car and looked up at the giant moon that hovered over the water, he remembered something. Her hair had been damp.

John found her on the beach immediately, almost as if he had known where to look. She lay half in and half out of the water. In the light of the moon she looked like a statue, or a painting of a person, instead of lifeless flesh and blood.

He pressed his hand to his heart again, remembering how it felt when she plunged her hand into his chest. He wondered what, if any, marks she had left on that fragile muscle.

Leave. Go now, John's thoughts cautioned him. *Leave her here.*

John walked across the uneven gravel and pulled her out of the water, trying to lift her in his arms. She was too heavy. When he let her go, her body rolled onto the gravel—one arm falling across her face.

Go now! screamed the voice in his head. *Go now and kill Aaron for what he's done.*

John shook his head. Why would Aaron do this? Why on earth would he hurt Katie?

He didn't want you to see her anymore, said the voice in a newly calm tone. *He's a killer. A monster.*

John looked up at the moon, because he couldn't look at her body for another moment. What had John done when he'd destroyed Katie's ghost? Had he also destroyed her soul? Was Katie really gone forever?

After a few moments, John opened his

bag and pulled out the wooden cigar box. He shook the bones into his hand.

"Pick her up," John said, looking out across the water, where the moon's reflection wavered. "Pick her up but don't hurt her. I don't want you to burn her."

John didn't know for sure that it would work, but he wasn't exactly surprised when the ghost with the goggles appeared. More relieved than anything. The ghost lifted Katie's body, almost tenderly, and walked up the path with John following close behind.

After John opened the trunk of the car, the ghost set Katie inside. Then the ghost stood there in silence, as though waiting for John to give another command. John looked where the man's eyes should have been. It was hard to tell how old the ghost had been when he died.

"How did you die?" John asked the man,

because he couldn't ask Katie. The ghost just shook his head and vanished.

John thought he might start to cry when he closed the trunk over Katie's cold body, but he didn't. Was she the sacrifice his uncle was talking about? Part of the ritual to keep the Portal closed? Was this what Aaron refused to tell him?

Yes, the voice insisted. *Aaron lies. He is a liar and a killer.*

As John started driving back to town, he suddenly felt calm, knowing that Aaron was going to pay for what he'd done.

At home, John parked the car in the driveway. He went inside and dropped his book bag in the front hall—just as he normally would after school. He then went upstairs and collapsed on his bed. He fell asleep almost instantly.

He dreamed of fire. A crackling, popping,

roaring fire that felt like a wall of heat in front of him. Within the dream he knew he had to walk through the fire, but he also knew that the fire would burn him alive. John took a step forward and felt the toes of his shoes start to smolder.

When John woke, he thought the dream was real because he could smell the smoke. John opened his eyes, not sure where he was for a moment. He often woke like that—blinking at the same walls he'd known all his life, but unable to recognize them for a few heartbeats. His mom once told him that, just after his father died, John used to wake up screaming.

John sat up and reached for the water on his nightstand. He drank and drank, but his mouth still somehow felt dry and sticky at the same time. Smoke. He definitely smelled smoke. John swung his legs out of bed.

As he walked barefoot across the hardwood floor, he stubbed his big toe on a broken floorboard. The board was warped and had come loose on one end. He'd been meaning to dig his dad's old toolbox out of the basement and put a few more nails in it.

John forgot, for those few moments, that Katie was still in the trunk of his car. When he remembered, he thought for an insane moment that she was the one who had started the fire. That Katie had climbed out of the trunk and was burning the whole house to the ground. But John knew that she was dead and that not even her ghost would be coming back.

Downstairs John found his mom kneeling before the woodstove, tending to a small fire. She had probably forgotten to open the flue, and the smoke was curling back into the living room.

"Mom?" He rubbed his eyes. "What time is it?" His mother didn't look up. "Go back to bed, John."

John walked slowly down the rest of the stairs. His head still felt groggy, like he saw everything a second after it happened.

His mom was wearing a threadbare robe with a long tear in the shoulder, right along the seam. She was holding a book in one hand, and was in the process of ripping out several pages, feeding them to the fire.

"What are you doing?" John ran over to her and pulled her away from the fireplace. He pried the book out of her hand, flinching when she slapped his face. He clutched the book to his chest. She didn't answer him, instead hanging her head and bending down to close the front of the stove.

His mother stood up slowly and wiped her hands on her legs. When she drew her robe

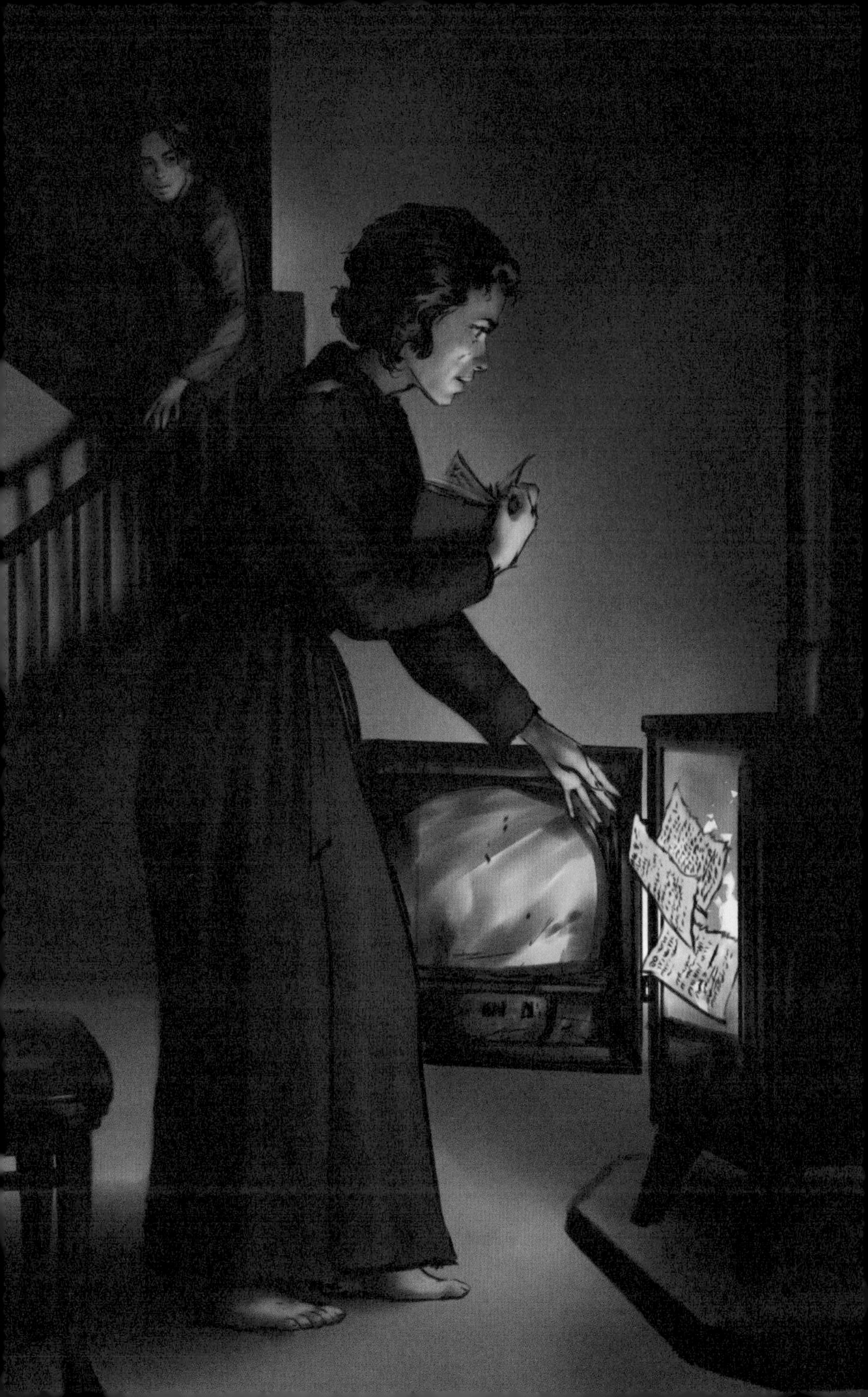

tighter around her waist, John noticed how thin his mother was—how sharp the bones of her face stood out in the firelight. He didn't know when she had gotten so skinny.

For one long, terrifying moment, John wondered if he was seeing his own mother's ghost. But then she went to him and put her arms around him.

"Mom?" John put his head on her shoulder. She smelled like smoke, but also like the perfume she always wore. Cloying and spicy—like flowers mixed with cinnamon. He pushed her away.

John flipped through the remaining pages of the partially-burned book, glancing at the familiar, handwritten words. It looked like only a few were missing. She must have just started to tear out pages when he came downstairs. He had come down in time— enough of it was left.

He realized in horror that he had left his book bag downstairs. His mother must have gone through it while he was sleeping. "What were you doing?" he asked. Looking around the room, John saw the gun, and the box of bones on the coffee table.

When his mother finally answered him, she turned away—her bony shoulders stiff and awkward. She was crying, John realized. He couldn't remember the last time he had seen her cry.

"I was trying to protect you from him. From this world." She gestured to the books, and the gun on the table. John almost went over and picked up the gun, too, but he fought the impulse. He couldn't threaten his own mother with a gun, and she would never use it against him. He was her son.

"You don't need to protect me from Aaron. I can take care of myself."

His mother shook her head, and didn't speak for a long while. Long enough that John noticed the light starting to shine through the windows. It must be morning.

Finally, she spoke. "I know why your father killed himself. It wasn't depression. I wasn't having an affair with your uncle." That was one of the stories that went around—that John looked too much like Aaron.

For a moment, John couldn't breathe. Which meant he almost couldn't ask the one question he had always wanted to know. Then he whispered, "Why?"

His mother looked at him with wide, sad eyes. "Because he thought there was a ghost inside him, and he was trying to save you."

chapter SEVEN

"What do you mean Dad had a ghost inside him?" John's head started to ache as he spoke—a sharp throbbing in his temples. "Ghosts don't just climb inside people."

His mother scrunched up her forehead, like she was trying to figure something out. Then she reached out her hand. "Can I see the journal again?"

John took a step back. "Absolutely not."

"I won't hurt it. I just . . . I want to show you something. Something your father showed me before he died."

John didn't give the book to his mother, but he held it out.

"Open it to the first page," she said. "Look at the inside of the cover."

John did as she asked. The words *Property of Ethan Hawthorne* were written there. "Who is Ethan?" he asked.

"Ethan was your great uncle. He was insane."

Lies.

John shook his head. "I've never heard of him before."

"Ethan died a long time ago. Do you remember the Accident? Ethan was there. The reason no one talks about him is because your grandfather wouldn't let them. He didn't want anyone to mention Ethan's name."

"Why?"

"Honey . . . your grandfather thought, for a long time, that Ethan caused the explosion. That he was somehow responsible. And there were other rumors at the time. Missing women. Well, your grandfather just started to pretend that his brother had never existed."

Lies. More lies. A deep, seething blackness roiled up from John's stomach. He tried to focus on his mother's words, but his head hurt so much. "But what does Ethan have to do with Dad?" John asked.

"Your father found this journal when he was a teenager. He became convinced that Ethan's ghost was in his head. Adam thought that Ethan had somehow gone into his body after the Accident. And it just got worse. Your father said that Ethan was telling him to do things. Bad things. Your father was afraid he was going to hurt you."

"Dad would never have hurt me."

"I know, honey. I know. But that's what your father thought. He would take out the journal and read it over and over again. The words made no sense. They were just crazy ramblings. Ethan was a disturbed man. And your father, well, he was obsessed with him.

In the end, well, I truly think he was trying to protect you."

"So it was my fault? I'm the reason he's dead?" John thought he would feel something when he said these words out loud—questions he had always wondered, but had never asked. But he just felt hollow.

His mom didn't answer at first. Her lower lip trembled when she said, "I didn't mean to blame you. That's why I didn't want you to know."

"But you do, don't you? You do blame me?"

"No," she said quickly, "I don't. I was just mad. Mad at your father. Mad at life. And I wondered . . . I couldn't help but wonder if there wasn't some truth to it. I looked for signs in you. Sometimes I thought . . ." she hung her head. "At times I was afraid. Afraid of my own son."

John stared at her.

"Can you forgive me?" she asked. Tears were running down her face. She looked so fragile. When John put his arms around her, he was uncomfortably aware of how breakable the bones that made up her rib cage were. How slight her neck.

Then John remembered Katie's body in the trunk of his car.

"Mom," John whispered, not entirely sure what words were about to follow. "Something bad happened." He had told his mother everything.

"We'll hide her body at Aaron's. Otherwise it will look like you did it," she said. John's mother was driving while he sat in the passenger seat.

"But it was Aaron," John said. "He killed Katie. I think it was part of a ritual. What if the ghost is inside Aaron? What if Ethan made him do it?"

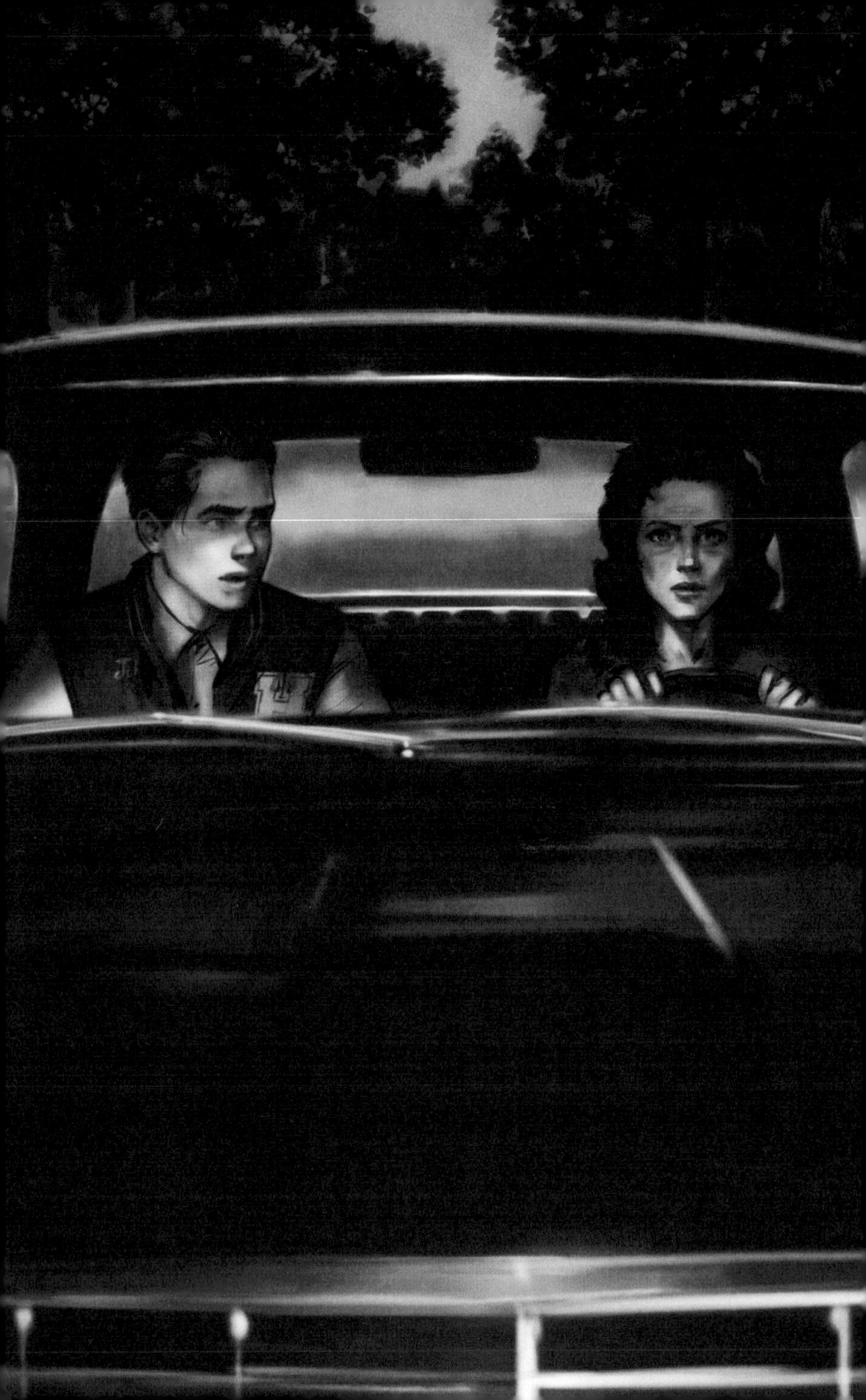

His mother had just nodded like she had expected it—like it was just one more piece of their inevitable future falling into place.

It took them almost an hour to dig a hole big enough, back behind the overgrown shrubbery in Aaron's front yard. They took turns shoveling. No one would ever look behind his uncle's big metal fence.

It was his mother who wrapped Katie in a blanket, and together they carried her body across the lawn to the newly dug grave. As the dirt covered Katie's body, John wondered why he didn't feel more—of anything. He just had an ache in his chest to do something. To go find Aaron.

Finally, John couldn't wait any longer. He left his mother to finish filling in Katie's grave and let himself into his uncle's house. He pulled the box of the ghost's bones out of his book bag and held it up like a weapon.

He found Aaron in his study. The room was dark, with just the soft, greenish light of the sun filtering through the leaves.

"I know your secret," John said, shaking the box of bones. "I know what you did."

John didn't really know what he expected. Perhaps that Aaron would finally explain everything. Why he kept the bones of a dead man in his library. Why he killed Katie.

Instead, Aaron closed the distance between them and slapped John hard across the face.

He'd been hit by his uncle before, but never so hard. His head whipped backward and slammed against the wall behind him.

"Boy," Aaron growled. "You think you can just play at something you don't understand? You think you can just take my things?"

Aaron wrapped both hands around John's neck and lifted him into the air. John sometimes forgot how incredibly strong his uncle was. He gripped Aaron's arms as his uncle shoved him across the room. He tried to speak—to tell him to let go, but he couldn't breathe. His uncle lifted John up and pressed his back against a shelf of books.

Right next to the ghost with the goggles. John could feel the ghost burning beside him. The edge of his vision lit up with the flames in the ghost's goggles. The bones rattled in their box—still clutched in John's hand—and the ghost flickered.

Aaron relaxed his hold on his nephew's neck, but held him firmly to the wall. "Do you have any idea what you took from my house?"

John's head was pounding again—worse than it had ever been. He felt like his brain was splitting down the middle. He cried out, tears streaming down his face, but his uncle just shook him.

"Do you know what you almost did?"

Aaron said. He released John, snatching the box of bones out of his hand. John fell to the floor, his vision blurring. Next to him, he could sense the ghost turn its attention to his uncle. The air around them grew hotter—so hot that John swore the tears on his face would turn to steam.

There was a movement outside the window. "John?" a voice called out. His mother. She had probably heard the yelling and was coming to see what had happened. Aaron turned toward the window, his back to John.

John saw an old paperweight that had been knocked from his uncle's desk in their struggle. It was shaped like a dog and was staring at him with its metallic, unblinking eyes. John reached out with a shaking hand and picked it up.

He stood on unsteady legs and lifted the paperweight—ready to strike his uncle's head.

Before he could bring it down, a scalding hand gripped John's wrist and twisted him around. The ghost with the goggles smiled at him. John screamed in pain. He could feel the fabric of his shirt burn against his skin, and the skin itself begin to blister.

Aaron turned back to John, holding up the cigar box triumphantly. He opened the lid and scooped up the shards of bone. They filled the palm of his hand. Half of John wanted to pass out, and let the pain be absorbed by the darkness. The other half held Aaron's gaze.

John didn't want to look at his arm, which had grown numb, like it wasn't even there.

"I won't let you do it," John said, though he didn't know what he meant by it, exactly. "I'll still stop you." He doubled over and threw up on his own shoes. He crouched there for what felt like a long time, shuddering and dry heaving.

He felt a hand on his back. "It's okay," Aaron was saying, "You're going to be just fine." Then John cried out in pain as his uncle pulled his arms sharply behind his back. The last thing he remembered before he passed out was the feeling of rope tightening around his wrists.

chapter EIGHT

On Friday, Jane woke in a terrible mood. She found herself frowning at her hands as she smoothed her stockings. She picked at an inflamed hangnail on her thumb and ripped it until a tiny bead of blood welled up.

Aaron had come over the night before, but she hadn't enjoyed herself—not the way she had on their first date. Jane had wanted to talk to Aaron about her day—about the newspaper clippings she had found.

Instead, Aaron gave her a bracelet and asked her to wear it the next day. It looked like it was made out of delicate pieces of white shell or ivory. He said that she was special. Then he said he was going to need her help. That she was going to help him make the world a better place. She was starting to wonder if Aaron was quite sane. When he left, Jane was left wondering what exactly had happened.

It started to pour down rain on the way to school. She had never seen clouds gather so quickly—the wind herding them across the sky like wayward sheep. When Jane arrived at school she found the students damp and bedraggled, and soon the room smelled like a combination of wet dog and soggy grass. Everyone was in a bad mood.

By third period Jane wanted to smother each and every one of her students. She was supposed to talk about the final days of World War II, but the children just kept talking over her.

"They're totally going to cancel the game," said one boy wearing a letterman's jacket. He didn't even bother to whisper. "This blows."

Jane raised her voice. "Can someone tell me what date the war officially ended?"

Another guy spoke up. "I think I saw lightning. Ah man, they're never going to let us on the field in a lightning storm."

"September second," Jane continued, talking over the top of her students. "The war ended on September second. Almost six years, exactly, from the beginning of the war."

When the lights went out, Jane felt as though time had slowed down, turned back upon itself— like she already knew it was going to happen. There were a few shrieks, and then nervous laughter from the class.

"All right," Jane said, standing up from where she had been leaning against her desk. "It is just a power outage from the storm. I want everyone to stay seated. Do not go near the windows." She imagined a tree branch shattering the glass and wondered if she should close the blinds. She gripped her hands together and turned the new bracelet over and over on her wrist.

"Miss Owens?" one of the girls said in a loud whisper.

"Yes?"

"I need to use the ladies' room."

"Me too," piped up another girl.

"Just stay in your seats," Jane commanded. There was utter silence for a full minute as Jane watched her class and the class watched her. Silence filled her ears until it became a hissing, rushing sound, like pressing your ear to a seashell.

When Jane was a senior in high school, they used to have duck-and-cover drills— as though their thin wooden desks could possibly protect them from a nuclear bomb. Still, as Jane faced her students, panic began to grip the base of her throat. Jane began to wonder if she should tell them to get under their desks and cover their heads.

When the screaming began, Jane flinched, but figured it was more nervous energy or some kids horsing around in the dark. But the screams didn't stop. They kept growing and spreading through the school, as fierce as the wind outside.

"Miss Owens?" It was the boy in the letterman's jacket.

"Yes?" She couldn't remember his name.

"I have to go." He pushed his chair back from the desk and was walking towards the door. "I just ... I can't stay here."

"Stay in your seat!" Jane snapped, hearing her voice grow shrill. The screaming kept getting louder, and she could hear running in the hallway. The boy opened the classroom door and was gone.

Jane hesitated for a moment. Should she

stay with her class or go after the boy? Finally, she told the other students, "If you get out of your seats, I will wring all of your necks." Then she left.

The hallway was dark, and there were students running past, though she couldn't see their faces. She jogged down the hall, trying to spot the boy's letterman's jacket among the students darting by. Someone slammed into her, and she was knocked off her feet, her head cracking against the floor. A foot stomped on her hand, and she cried out, scooting toward the wall.

She sat there—covering her head with her hands, listening to the pounding footsteps of terrified students. Then she smelled it. Smoke. It was faint at first—just a tinge of something acrid in the back of her nose and a faint stinging in her eyes.

Fire. The realization hit her like a slap

in the face. She started to cough, and she couldn't stop until her lungs felt bloody. Jane's first thought was to run to the front door, out to her car, and drive home. Drive as far as she could from this school. This whole town.

Then Jane tried to remember the proper procedures. Surely there should be an alarm going off, and the students should evacuate the building. But the only sounds Jane heard were the screams and the footfalls of children running every which way in the dark.

Jane pushed herself up and pressed her back against the wall. The smoke was growing thicker, and she could feel heat on the left side of her face, in the direction of her classroom. It was impossible to see in the dark and the smoke, but she could just make out an orange glow down the hall. When she heard the first real voice of the fire, the crackling and the whoosh of flame, Jane ran.

She pushed her way through a mob of students who had gathered at the front door. Jane elbowed and shouldered her way to the front, until her hand was on the handle. As the skin of her hand stuck to the white-hot metal, Jane screamed.

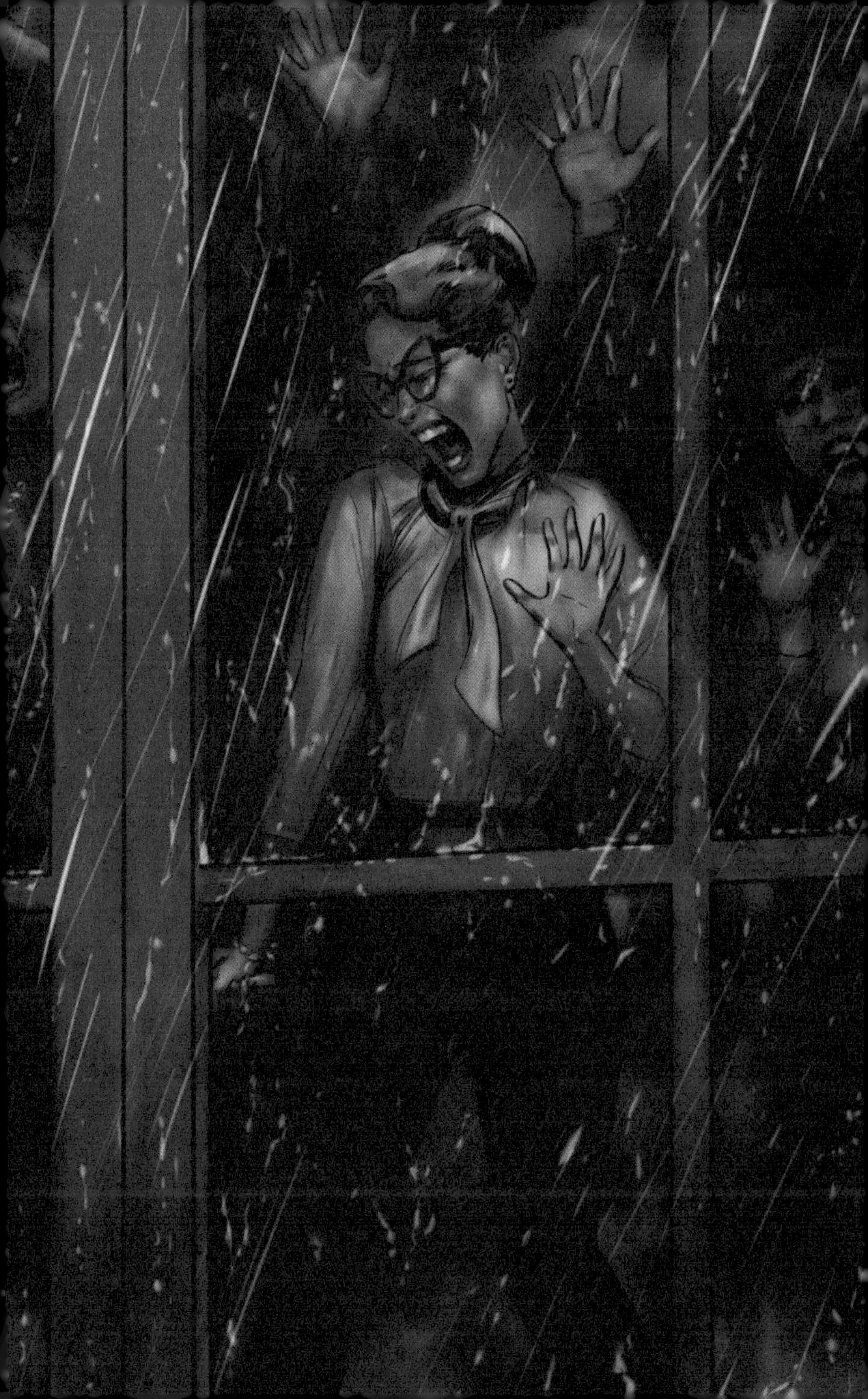

chapter NINE

When John woke up, he was at home in bed. His mother was sitting beside him. He tried to sit up, but his hands were tied to the bed. He looked at his mother. "What's happening?"

"John," she began, placing a hand on his forehead, "it's to keep you safe. Aaron explained it to me." Her eyes were rimmed with red. "Would you like a glass of water?"

Too late! Oh God, I'm too late! John didn't know why he was thinking those words, or why he was filled with bitter regret. It felt like someone had punctured a hole in his body, and he was draining out of himself. "What day is it? What time?"

"It's Friday. Almost noon. But sweetheart,

like I said, Aaron already explained everything. He's just trying to keep you alive."

"Let me go!" It wasn't too late after all. There was still time. Not much, but a few hours. Time enough to stop Aaron. These thoughts in his head cut through his skull like the blade of a pickaxe, and tears sprang to his eyes as his head throbbed and his vision blurred.

His mother shook her head. "I won't. I'm not letting you go." Her eyes filled with tears again, and John could see she was exhausted. "I'm not letting you die, too."

"Mother!" He struggled against the ropes. His shoulder still hurt, but it was a little better. "Mother, this isn't your decision to make. You have to let me go. Now. Or more people are going to die."

She nodded. "I know, honey. But not you."

"Let me go!" he shouted, pulling at his

binds until his wrists started to bleed. "You don't understand. Let me go!"

There was a loud snap, and one of the wooden bars of John's bed broke away. As his mother stared in horror, John untied his other wrist, and jumped out of bed, the rope still clutched tightly in his hand.

"Don't," she said, holding her hands out in front of her. "Don't do this."

"You made me do this," John heard himself say. "You should have let me go."

Quiet John—the John who usually waited in the back of his mind and watched—that John grabbed his mother by the arm and wrapped the rope around her neck.

Stop it, John thought to himself, feeling like he was in a terrible dream. *Stop it now.* But he couldn't stop it, even as his mother clawed at his arms. Even as her body went limp and collapsed to the floor. Even then he twisted the rope, until her lips turned blue.

John changed his clothes, putting on a clean pair of jeans and a new shirt. He watched himself get dressed, with his mother's body lying in a heap behind him.

Downstairs, the journal and the gun were still sitting on the coffee table, right where he had left them before they left to bury Katie's body. He had to hide the journal. Someone might take it from him. Someone might try to hurt it again.

Hurry, said the voice while he frantically looked for a hiding place. *We have to hurry.*

When he was done, John took the gun and went outside. Not seeing his car in the driveway, he started to run through the pouring rain.

It would take him less than ten minutes to get to school. He could still make it. He still had time. He glanced at his wrist as he ran.

Where is my watch? John thought, not sure why it was suddenly so important. *Where is my watch?*

Come on, come on, rang a louder voice in his head, drowning out John's thoughts. *Hurry. We have to hurry!* As John ran, his mind went blessedly blank.

When he got to the school, he could tell the ritual had already started. He could see the flickering light of the fire in the windows. He needed to get inside. He needed to find Aaron. John closed his eyes, and thought, *Where would he be?*

By the Portal, the voice said—no longer a whisper, but as clear as if someone were standing beside him in an empty room. *He has to be by the Portal.*

"Where?" John said aloud. "Where is the Portal?"

Find him.

John ran, rain dripping into his eyes. He looked for an open window—somewhere he could get in. Finally, he found a broken window on the far side of the school, near the gym. He climbed in, almost slicing his leg on the glass. In the distance, he heard sirens.

He ran down the hallway squinting against the many fires that seemed to have sprung up independently in each room. It was the work of the ghost, he somehow knew. The ghost with the goggles. *Wesley Owens*, the voice told him. *That fool.*

John suddenly found himself wondering how Aaron had created such a powerful Token, one that could not only control the ghost but also feed him. Make him stronger.

"Where are you, Aaron?" John yelled, but he couldn't remember forming the words. "Where are you?" The smoke was so thick that John had to close his eyes. Somehow, he could still see—still make his way down the hall—now empty of students. They must all be hiding somewhere. Or burning. He had to stop Aaron. This was madness.

As he ran, John kept seeing his mother's face, pleading with him. He kept seeing Katie's body. John had a flash of a memory— he saw his watch shattering on smooth, round stones. He could feel nails clawing at his hands. Not just his mother's hands, but Katie's as well.

Not now. Don't think of them now. Just run. John did what the voice told him.

He ran.

All around, people were burning. Jane ran back toward her classroom, not knowing what else to do. She glanced inside Mr. Benson's room and saw what looked like a pillar of flame by the front desk. Her stomach turned, and she tasted bile. She kept running.

At first, Jane thought that her room was empty, but then she saw the little forms huddled beneath their desks.

"There is a fire," she rasped, her voice shot from all the coughing and screaming. "You need to get up, now." Her hand was bleeding from when she ripped it off the handle, and it was curled in a sort of half-claw at her side. Useless. She didn't even really feel it anymore.

"Get up!" she repeated, overturning one of the desks in the front row. A girl shrieked and scooted back into the arms of a girl behind her.

"We're going to burn to death!" Jane shouted. At the back of the room, the wall was covered in flame. She got down low, trying to breathe beneath the smoke, and made her way over to the window. She tried to open the window but it wouldn't budge. "We have to break it," she wheezed, picking up a chair and throwing it against the glass. Jane couldn't even hear the sound of the glass breaking over the roar of the fire. It was going to be too late, she realized, watching the fire multiply and consume the back half of the room.

"Come on!" Jane shrieked, pulling one of the girls with her. "Get out!" She tried to lift the girl through the window, but the girl struggled and kicked her in the stomach. "Now!" Jane shouted. "Get out now!" There was a loud whoosh, and the girl exploded into flame. Her brown hair fizzled into nothing, and Jane could see her features cracking and blackening. Jane could see her eyes burst.

The flame that consumed the girl whooshed up the side of Jane's arm and neck. Jane screamed, knowing that this was her last moment—the last sound that would come from her lips. She lifted her arm to her face and screamed, "No!"

And then it stopped. Jane could still see the flames dance over her skin—licking over her strange bracelet and eating her clothes. But it wasn't burning her anymore. She stared at the bracelet in the flickering, wild light of the fire. It seemed to writhe and pulse on her wrist like a living thing, almost in time with the flames themselves.

There must be music, she thought suddenly—madly. *Music I can't hear.*

Jane laughed—because what else was there to do?—and then coughed and coughed as she breathed in the smoke. Was she dead? Was she a ghost? But she didn't feel dead. Her burns didn't even hurt anymore, but perhaps they were just too big a pain to feel.

She looked back at her students one more time, as they writhed and burned around her, and she ran out the door. Jane felt light—her soul had burned to dust, but her body was

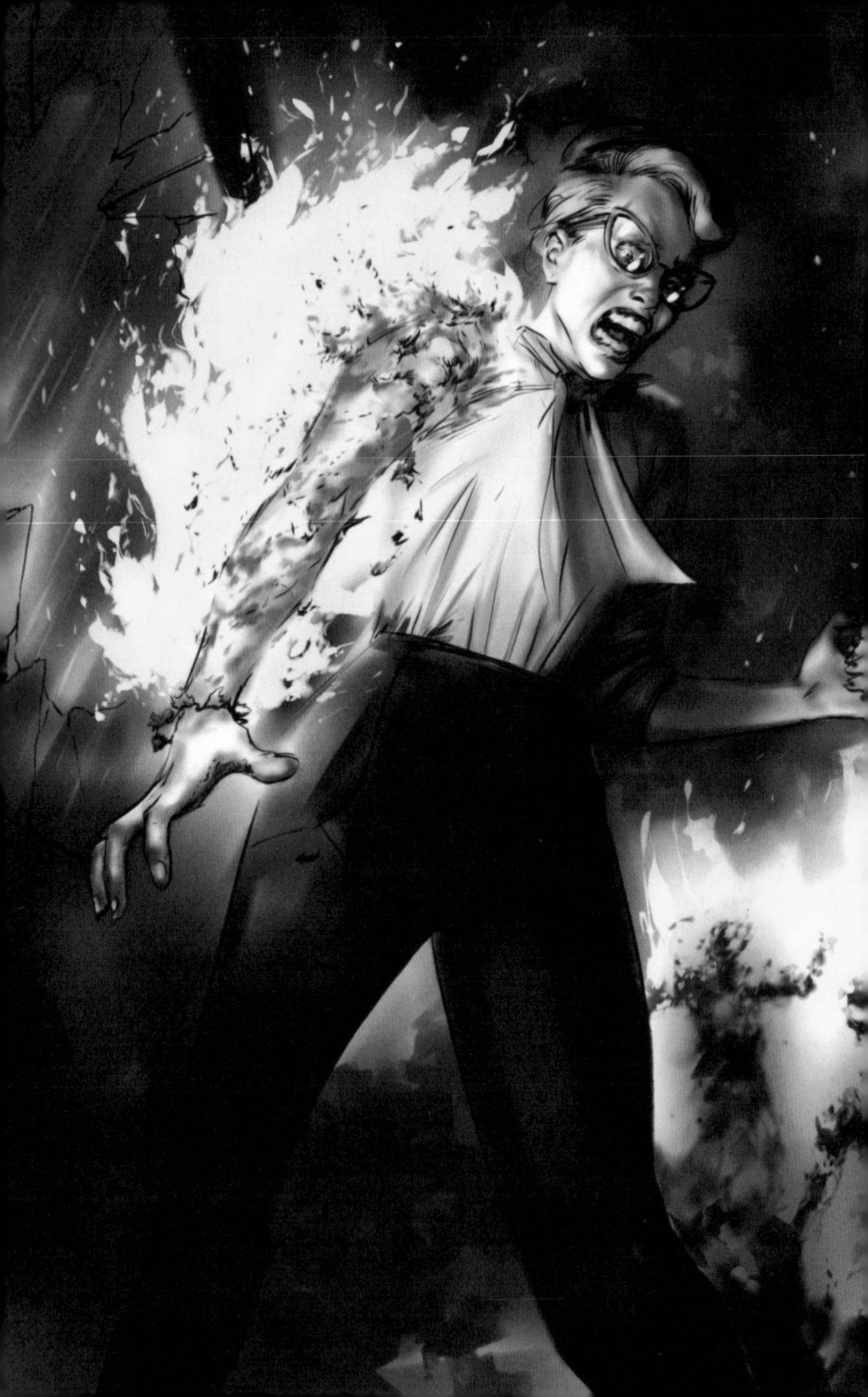

still whole. She held her breath and ran down the burning hallway, looking in each room. Trying to find anyone else who was alive.

chapter
TEN

John found his uncle standing in the center of the gymnasium. He was holding his hands above his head, and his eyes were closed. The flames hadn't reached this part of the school yet, but it was just a matter of time.

"Stop it," he yelled to his uncle. "Stop the ritual."

Aaron opened his eyes. In the dark of the gym, Aaron was surrounded by an orange glow. "I can't. It's too late." John saw that Aaron had his right hand clenched into a fist, and he realized that his uncle was holding the ghost's bones. He was making the ghost do this.

John raised the gun and pointed it at his uncle's chest. Even though he had never fired a gun, he had that feeling again that when he pulled the trigger, he wouldn't miss. "Tell the ghost to stop." John's voice echoed across the room.

"I wanted to save you from this, John. I had hoped it would be different for you than for your father. But Ethan's too strong, isn't he? Even after everything I taught you. You'll never be free of him. I can see that now."

Aaron raised his hand and gestured toward the gun. In an instant, the gun was so hot that John dropped it. It spun away from him and toward the door.

"You can't stop me," John shouted. His head hurt worse than it ever had before. It felt as though a hand was reaching out through his skull. He doubled over in agony. "You haven't won yet." As he spoke the words that he realized, finally, did not belong to him, John saw a light out of the corner of his eye. A bright, thin line that flickered between him and his uncle.

John heard himself laugh. "See! It wasn't enough! The Portal is opening!"

Aaron shook his head, walking toward John. "You never did know what you were doing, Ethan. That's why my father beat you. The Portal isn't opening. It is accepting the sacrifice."

John screamed—Ethan's voice ripping out of his throat. "Adam killed himself because of you. Did you know that, Aaron? Your own brother didn't think you could beat me."

"John," Aaron shouted back, "if you can still hear me, you need to fight Ethan. You need to run. Get out of here."

John's whole body was shaking as he tried to take control back from the other, angry John. The John that he now realized was not really John at all, but was a ghost that lived inside him. It was Ethan. Ethan Hawthorne.

He focused on his uncle's face. John trembled when he said, "I killed her. I killed my mother. I think I killed Katie." He gasped a huge, racking sob and felt his body double over. But when he stood back up, Ethan was back in control.

Aaron's face was stricken. "You killed them? Susan's dead?"

"Does it matter?" Ethan said. "You're killing hundreds of people. And for what? To put off the inevitable for another fifty years? I'll keep coming back. I will beat you, eventually."

"But not yet," Aaron said, taking hold of John as he struggled against the ghost. Aaron pulled out a knife and held it to John's throat. "I'm so sorry, John. I hope you can forgive me someday."

Another memory flashed through John's mind's eye. Katie's face beneath a veil of water.

Katie's eyes wide and frightened—staring up at him.

"Do it. Please," John whispered, fighting to use his own voice. "Ethan. He's too strong."

When Jane reached the gym she saw two things. First, she saw Aaron holding a knife to his nephew's throat. Then she saw a gun at her feet. She picked the gun up and held it with her burned hand. Her father had taught her to use a gun when she was a teenager—one of the few useful things he had passed along to her.

"Let go of him," she called out to Aaron. Jane didn't understand what she was seeing. Why would Aaron try to kill John? His own nephew? But the world was burning around her, and nothing made sense.

"Jane," Aaron said, glancing from the gun to her face. "Put that down. You have no idea what is happening right now."

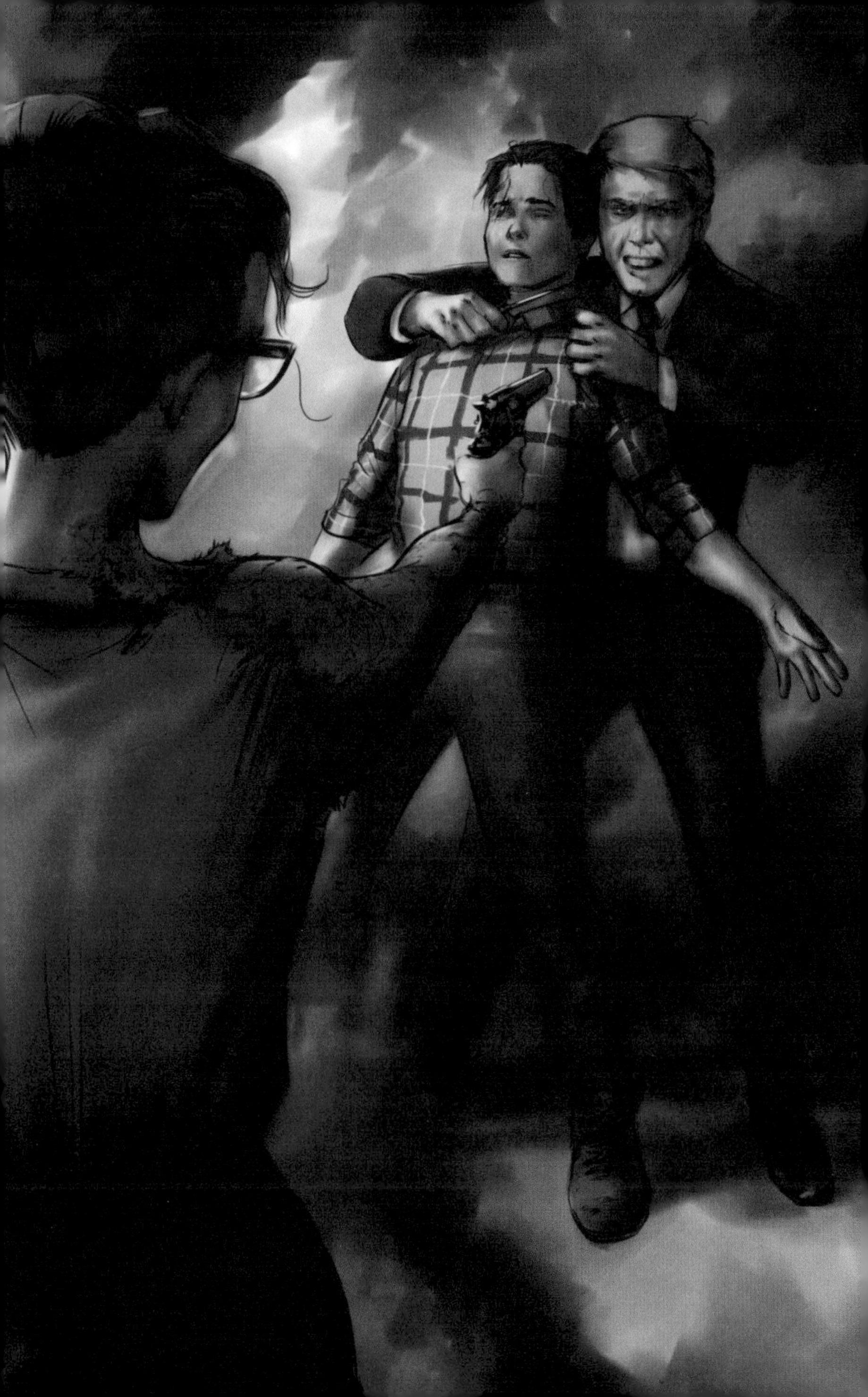

John looked like he wanted to speak, but the knife was pressed so close to his Adam's apple that he might just slit his own throat if he tried.

"Drop him," she said again, bringing the gun level with Aaron's eyes.

"You won't shoot me, Jane dear. I know you won't. I have to do this." When Aaron moved his hand, Jane pulled the trigger. She screamed at the deafening gunshot, but her aim was steady.

John tried to scream, "No!" But it was too late. As his uncle died, Aaron's lifeless arms released him. As John watched his uncle drop to the floor of the gym, he felt Ethan take control of his body again. He watched himself pick up the knife and approach the teacher.

"Are you okay?" Miss Owens asked him, lowering the gun. "Did he hurt you?"

When John sliced her arm, she dropped

the gun. "What are you doing?" Her voice was a thin croak, and she started to cough. John wanted to stop—to let Miss Owens leave before Ethan killed her too.

John tried to pull his hand back, and he was able to stop the knife, just for a moment. Just long enough, he hoped.

Jane held her hands in front of her face, waiting for John's knife to strike her. When it didn't, she looked up and saw a figure standing behind John. It was Aaron.

Again Jane struggled to make sense of what she was seeing. Aaron's body was still lying right where it had fallen when she shot him between the eyes. But there he was standing right behind his nephew. A bloody hole oozed darkly in the middle of his forehead.

Aaron smiled. He reached out his hand and took hers, just like he had that first day, after she fell asleep at school.

Time seemed to stop when he raised her hand to his lips. He kissed her hand. Then, he vanished.

John growled and swung the knife toward her face. Jane's instinct was to back up and cover her eyes, but she heard herself scream, "Grab his arm!"

John's arm stopped in mid-swing, and his face contorted into something ugly.

She took a step forward, and her head began to pound. "Take him to the Portal," she yelled, pointing to the center of the gym. *Everything is going to be all right*, said a voice in her head. A voice that sounded exactly like Aaron's. *I'll take care of everything.*

Something Jane couldn't see dragged John backwards, until he appeared to totter on the back of his heels.

"This won't stop me!" John shouted, struggling against his unseen captor. "You're still going to fail." Then John vanished.

Jane could just make out a thin, watery light where John had been standing. Then, for a brief fraction of a second, she saw another person standing in front of the light. Even though the man was wearing dark welder's goggles, Jane knew he was looking right at her.

He smiled, and in that moment, he looked almost exactly like her father. She stared at him, the tears she had refused to cry before coming unbidden to her eyes.

Then he was gone.

Jane knew she needed to get out of there. She needed to run, and keep running, until she was far away from here. But instead, she stood there and, despite the tears running down her cheeks, smiled to herself.

She felt for the bracelet on her wrist and turned it around and around.

"I'm here, Jane," she heard herself say. But it wasn't her voice. Deep in the back of her mind, she could hear Aaron saying each word.

"*Everything is going to be okay. You'll never have to be alone again.*"